EAL 5.85

Susan Goldman

Grandpa and Me Together

Albert Whitman & Company, *Chicago*

Also by Susan Goldman
Grandma Is Somebody Special
Cousins Are Special

J
G

Copyright © 1980 by Susan Goldman Rubin
Published simultaneously in Canada
by General Publishing, Limited, Toronto
All rights reserved. Printed in U.S.A.

Library of Congress Cataloging in Publication Data

Goldman, Susan
  Grandpa and me together.

  (A Self-starter book)
  SUMMARY: Katherine spends the day doing
special things with her grandfather.
  [1. Grandfathers—Fiction] I. Title.
PZ7.G5693Gs   [E]   79-18244
ISBN 0-8075-3036-0 lib. bdg.

For Michael
with love

When I stay at Grandpa's, he's
the first one up in the morning.

He sings a good morning song to me.
"Good morning to you,
Good morning to you,
Good morning, dear Katherine,
Good morning to you."

Then he makes orange juice with the juicer.

"Grandpa, can I help?" I ask.

"Sure you can, big girl," he says.

I hold the orange and Grandpa
turns on the switch.
"This juicer comes from
my old store," says Grandpa.
"Can we go there?" I ask.
"Maybe today," says Grandpa.

When Grandma gets up we make her
a glass of orange juice.
"Today I'm going to an art show," she says.

"Katherine and I are going to visit my old store," says Grandpa. "Then we'll go to the ball game."
"Hooray!" I shout.

When we get into Grandpa's car I
wave goodbye to Grandma. I look
out the window as we drive downtown.

Everyone at Grandpa's old store
knows him.

"Hello, Morey," says a man.

"Good to see you."

"Hi, Walt. Hi, Ella," says Grandpa.

"This is my granddaughter, Katherine."

"Morey, we're having a problem in shipping," says Walt. "Can you help us for a minute?"
"Sure," says Grandpa.

While Grandpa is gone, Ella lets
me type on her typewriter.
"How do you spell 'Grandpa'?" I ask.
"G-R-A-N-D-P-A," says Ella.

I write, "I love you, Grandpa."
Then I draw hearts and stars
on the paper.

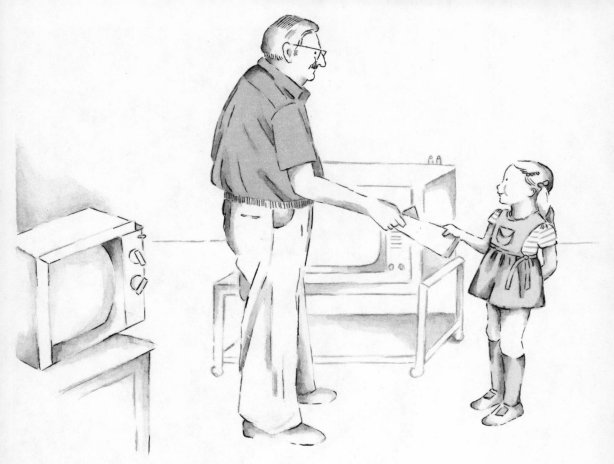

When Grandpa comes back,
I give him the letter.
"Thank you, sweetheart," he says.
"I'll keep this forever."

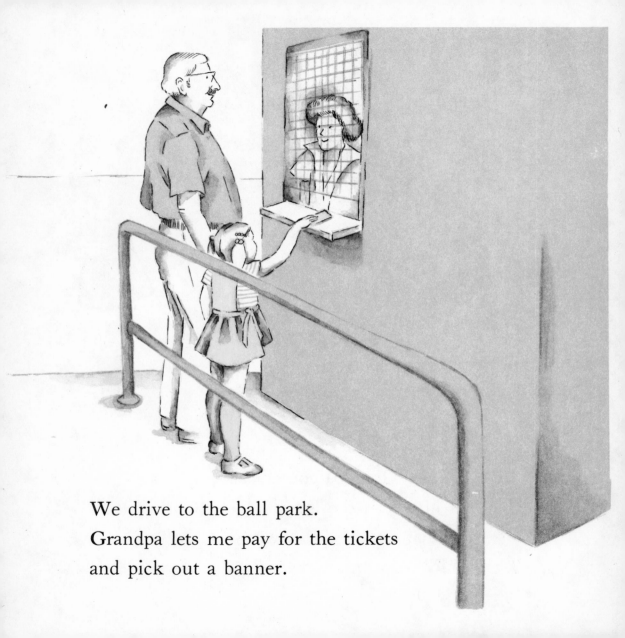

We drive to the ball park.
Grandpa lets me pay for the tickets
and pick out a banner.

I hold the banner while I watch
all the people watching the game.

"Peanuts, hot dogs," shouts a man.
"Grandpa, I'm hungry," I say. "Are you?"
Grandpa gives me money, and I go
to buy our hot dogs.

"One with ketchup and one with
mustard," I say. "And a bag of
peanuts, please."
Grandpa and I eat while we watch
the game.

Suddenly everyone jumps up.
They yell and cheer.
"What happened, Grandpa?"
"It's a home run," he says.
"Our team won the game."

On the way home Grandpa tells me
how he played baseball in college.
He teaches me his college song,
and we sing it together.

"Here's to Michigan we sing,
With a merry, merry ring,
As we gaily roll along,
We will sing this merry song."

When we get home Grandpa shows
me the picture of him in his
baseball uniform.
"You look different," I say.
"He was younger and skinnier,"
says Grandma.

"I weighed one hundred and thirty-nine
pounds wringing wet," says Grandpa.
"How much do I weigh
wringing wet?" I ask.
"Take a bath before dinner and find
out," says Grandma.

After my bath I get on the scale.
"Grandpa, I weigh forty-three
pounds wringing wet," I shout.

"You're sure getting big, big girl,"
says Grandpa as he powders my toes.
"When I'm big enough, can I go
to your college, too?"
Grandpa gives me a hug.
"Of course," he says.

"Good," I say. "Because
I already know the song."
And Grandpa and I sing it
for Grandma one more time.